THE WORLD
AND HUMANS

THE WORLD AND HUMANS

DEJAN STOJANOVIĆ

Translated by
Željko Mitić

New Avenue Books

&

 ALBATROS PLUS

THE WORLD AND HUMANS
English translation Copyright © 2024 New Avenue Books

This book was originally published in Serbia, Belgrade, in 2017 by UKS (The Association of Writers of Serbia) under the title *The World and Humans* (*Svet i ljudi*) as the fourth book in the pentalogy *The World in Nowhereness* (Pentalogy: *Ozar, The World and God, The World in Nowhereness, The World and Humans, The Home of light*). (Serbian: *Svet u nigdini* - Pentalogija: *Ozar, Svet i Bog, Svet u nigdini, Svet i ljudi, Dom svetlosti.*).

New Avenue Books
&
Albatros Plus

First Edition in English

Library of Congress Control Number: 2024950271

ISBN-13: 979-8-9916352-8-8

THEY SAID ABOUT *THE WORLD IN NOWHERENESS*

"When I got my hands on Dejan Stojanović's book *The World in Nowhereness*, I was amazed and read the book with great pleasure. I did not even believe there was someone today who could write such a long poem, an epic, as if I opened to read the *Iliad* in our time. I recommend this book to all believers in poetry because faith in poetry is the same as faith in eternity and eternal life."

— *Matija Bećković*

"*The World in Nowhereness* is Dejan Stojanović's utopian absolute book, a Mallarméan absolute. An absolute story, or an absolute book, according to Borges, is a desert-like book: sandy, grainily unforeseeable, and corpuscularly innumerable. It is simultaneously a vision and a chimera. Isn't that precisely why we long for an absolute book? *The World in Nowhereness* by Dejan Stojanović is, in his way, an embodiment of that dream."

— *Srba Ignjatović*

"I have always wondered, even about my poetic work, what a total poem is… Can the pentalogy by Dejan Stojanović be called a total poem that every poet of note has dreamed about since Homer? I felt such impulses while reading *The World in Nowhereness*. This is an absolute poem, of an absolute system of thought that reaches across the totality of our civilizational legacies."

— *Duško Novaković*

"Exactly 17 years ago, in the last year of the 20th century, I came across the work of Dejan Stojanović, and then I wrote a text from which I will extract a few sentences. "Dejan Stojanović, in the last two years, made a real feat; he published six books, except for one, all books of poetry." This first five-book collection was published in the last year of the 20th century, and here we are now with the five-book collection in the XXI century, nearing the end of the second decade. And then I also wrote the following: "Stojanović is a poet who searches for the perfect poetic form because at the same time he searches for the absolute meaning of human existence." Whether it was a hunch or not, there is the Pentalogy, and there is that word, that concept – an absolute, an absolute book, an absolute poem that could be sensed even in that first pentalogy, in those poems that he published at that time."

— *Aleksandar Petrov* (January 17, 2018)

"(*The World in Nowhereness* offers) the joy of cognition due to discoveries worthy of the Nobel Prize…"

— *Milan Lukić*

"*The World in Nowhereness* is primarily the result of great literary ambition and faith in literature. It was not only Kiš who said that literature is created by form and that Sartre's quote should be placed at the entrance to the Association of Serbian Writers that "someone does not become a writer to say certain things, but to say them in a certain way." Dejan Stojanović is one of those who think well about that way and think very sovereignly and broadly. Even in how he approaches the form, we can see the breadth of his education, including the humanities and the natural sciences. However, perhaps more than anything else, he enters into some area of spirituality and, I would even dare say, esoteric. If you read Dejan Stojanović, your life will not be the same – it will be better."

— *Muharem Bazdulj*

"It has been quite a while since we had, if at all, a poetic pentalogy in Serbian poetry."

— *Dušan Stojković*

Dejan Stojanović's poetic-philosophical book *The World in Nowhereness*, both in form and content, is an original and exceptional literary work and can be considered a rare literary event in Serbian poetry and on the world stage.

— *Nevena Vitošević*

"It is every poet's dream to write a relevant, unique, comprehensive book in which he will properly present all his thoughts and feelings that have appeared in his long conversations with the world. By the *world,* I mean everything manifested and abstract in (a) language, what is named, and what can be named. Dejan Stojanović's extensive pentalogy *The World in Nowhereness* is an attempt at writing such a book. This pentalogy about the world and light is an ambitious endeavor."

— Bratislav R. Milanović

"*The World in Nowhereness*, the pentalogy by Dejan Stojanović, is an unusual endeavor in Serbian literature."

— Nikola Marinković

"*The World in Nowhereness*, a poetic endeavor by Dejan Stojanović, is an exceptional occurrence in Serbian."

— Dragan Kolarević

"There are very few such books in Serbian literature."

— Ivan Cvetanović

"(The publishing of *The World in Nowhereness* is) a significant date in contemporary Serbian poetry."

— Miljurko Vukadinović

"Steadfast and consistent, with his mapping out of circular trajectories in the realms of poetry and philosophy, and always being something more than the sum of all parts, Dejan Stojanović has proved to be a thinker of continuously inventive thought. He belongs to that creative ilk whose body of work affirms the permanence of the long-established unity of the Mystic and the Magus. On the one hand, he is one of those with extensive knowledge and who, according to Bela Hamvash, are Mystics. Yet, he is also one of the Magi, who also possesses knowledge, but one meant to encourage and reflect the urge to peer into the other, lesser-known or completely unexplored side, which light cannot reach at first glance."

— David Kecman Dako

Dejan Stojanović, a sincere devotee of both poetry and philosophy, achieved a real poetic feat in 2017 by publishing an extensive five-volume book titled *The World in Nowhereness*.

— Aleksandar B. Laković

"The author is deeply immersed in his attempt to decode the essence of the universe, the meaning of the origin, and the persistence of being therein. He seeks balance and the possibility of introducing harmony into seemingly incompatible, disharmonious phenomena and concepts."

— *Gordana Vlahović*

"Dejan Stojanović offers us *The World in Nowhereness*, his latest book, as a spiritual anthology. This is an ambitious poetic and essayistic project in a predominantly philosophical, dense, and layered pentalogy about humanity as the source and the final destination of all visible and invisible worlds. The manuscript is presented in innovative, avant-garde form. Dejan Stojanović wisely and expertly intertwines poetry and prose, the epic and the lyrical, and the theoretical-critical."

— *Zorica Arsić Mandarić*

"Stojanović's pronounced contemplativeness is what makes him stand out in the contemporary world of the poetic invention as one of the few being in no quandary about the equality of poetry and philosophy and the necessity of their proper understanding, as well as a deeper decoding of the meaning behind words. For that reason, I see his search in the book *The World in Nowhereness* as a quest for the meaning of elemental survival in a time that is alienated, brutally real, and preoccupied with everything and nothing."

— *Vidak Maslovarić*

"Stojanović's poetic, prosaic, and dramatic approach represents, in a unique sense, an array of basic concepts and elements of human existence, its earthly and cosmic destiny. He tackles the subjects of freedom, the Absolute, God, the Devil, chaos, order, truth, the world, etc. The philosophical, the religious, and the poetic make up the basic core in the interpretation and understanding of the ontology of human survival."

— *Jovo Cvjetković*

Contents

THE WORLD AND HUMANS

MEDITATIONS

THE SUN AND SEA STARS

Only the sea can bring urchins and stars together,
Black thorns and white stars in the infinity of blue;
Plenty of black seaweed and scents of the sea and stone.
A shell resting against the ear –
A music box concealing
The secret hum of the universe and its notes
And we are playfully merging
With the sea, the sky, sea stars
And urchins, while forgetting about boundaries,
Divisions, and feeling that we're breathing,
Observing and being here,
Here, with the Sun visiting us.
Single color in various shades – one world.

THE SEA AND THE SKY

Nowhere is there a more vital link to the sky than at sea. Although the land and the sea are equally distant from the sky, the sea nearly touches it, not only with its color but with a weightless weight that erases boundaries.

The sound and smell of the sea speak of the origin and links among various realities, both the visible life and the hidden and submerged one. The sea reveals the truth and its secret, something we love and fear, something that rewards and punishes. The sea touches infinity, and a conversation with it is a conversation with infinity.

All it takes is to lie in the seawater, start to swim, and experience a stronger touch of the universe. At the same time as the swimmer performs strokes in the sea, he is swimming in an immense sea and through a more extensive vault, unconsciously experiencing the unity of the world.

THE SEA AND SILENCE

Near water, the air is also different, and silence is less mysterious. Water is a fluid that connects worlds and helps silence open. Near water, the world opens up, and silence begins to speak. It's a silence that reveals both day and night. A silence that has heard many secrets and witnessed shipwrecks and the birth and submergence of shores. Silence brings the world to the surface.

Silence speaks of the secret of water, the way water speaks of life; silence counts the waves and listens to inaudible words. In silence, the unborn sea, from which the sea is born, sleeps; an eternal sea that hides all waves and all letters.

Silence conceals the whole reality, each past and future moment. Silence is the sum of all sounds, the world of all worlds. It is immortal; deceased images live on in it. Silence is the invisible radar of the world, its library and cinematheque. The world springs from silence and flows into it.

There is no greater source than silence, nor a more generous interlocutor if one knows how to approach and court her, so she opens up and starts talking without words in a language known to those who see the value of silence and cherish her treasures. To open silence is to open the world.

SHORES

There are no two shores nor countless shores. There is but one shore. What gives meaning to the shore and what connects all shores is a path. A shore is lost in its void without a void or a space that enables a path. The path is a shore that connects all shores, joining them into one. Only the path provides value to the shores.

All shores make one; all paths merge into one. A shore has no meaning without another looking for it, longing for it while being struck by the waves of infinity. The goal is not another shore or a port. The path is the goal.

MEDITATION

We need to listen to nature and water, close our eyes for a moment, and surrender to the inner peace that listens to the inaudible sound of the universe with which we merge. To become, for a moment, one with the world.

Sometimes, all it takes are a few moments of silence, a cup of tea, and listening to the waves. To close our eyes and the peace that moves into our soul erases the inner restlessness. We become one with the world without the need to prove anything or compete in a world where every victory becomes our accomplishment.

We hear the wave of the sea inside, the inaudible sound of the river flowing through us; we hear the world that has a muffled conversation with us. The whole world becomes our interlocutor. The path to oneself is the path to the soul of the world.

THE STELLAR WASTE

As long as it lives, a star is the simplest celestial body. All the fire of the Sun radiates from two elements. The source of life and the source of all elements blazes with the fire of simplicity. The death of a star is the beginning of a new life – with its death, it gives birth to life. The fertilizer of life is the waste of the stellar fire – carbon, oxygen, zinc, gold, silver. Life emerges from soot; an extinguished fire flows through our veins. A butterfly, centipede, lion are stellar decay's fruits. Life sprouts in the starry midden, in the machinery of disintegration and processing of elements. In purity, life is impossible – waste feeds it. Purity is sterile – it feeds life but is not life. Purity is the source of the world, and waste is its life.

VARIOUS DIMENSIONS

Nothing separates us from the world except for the senses that explain and touch it and give it shape, color, and meaning. Every dimension of the world is concealed within us, and so is every secret. Knowing the biology of the world is equally important and can lead to conclusions similar to those obtained from knowing its physics, metaphysics, cosmology, and cosmogony.

> There is neither a top nor a bottom
> Neither end nor beginning
>
> There is no sky
> Or Earth (as we see them)
>
> There is no light
> Or color (except sight)
>
> We are both top and bottom
> Both color and light
>
> We are space and time
> We are motion
>
> There are no various dimensions
> Only various experiences of the very same
>
> World that is happy to see us

Matter, dark matter, dark energy, antimatter are everywhere, in every physical form. An ant is a biological universe for itself, with microgalaxies orbiting its cells and atoms. The whole world is the flow and flutter of an invisible and elusive fluid.

INFINITY

We are always looking for infinity outside, fantasizing about an endless space of galaxies, cosmoses, and other cosmoses that contain smaller ones within. Meanwhile, in the spiral of the Cosmos, there are not only billions of galaxies but also billions of cosmoses. Infinity, too, remains equally distant. Unsolvable, incomprehensible – trapped in its infinity, which traps us and drives us crazy. This game of infinity, and with infinity in infinity, is without prospect. In this game, we are destined to lose.

The path toward infinity is the pursuit of the end, not of infinity. Infinity drives us crazy with the very impossibility of definition, the impossibility of identifying the boundary, the end. The path toward infinity is equally long if one goes in or if one goes out, if one searches for oneself in galaxies or in atoms.

One contains innumerability within, and innumerability contains One. Reaching the inner end of the One, or the small, is as complicated and distant as reaching the end of innumerability, or the big. Infinity is within us, and so is the answer. Reaching the end of the path of each of our atoms is as difficult as reaching the end of the universe. The end of our infinity is equally incomprehensible. However, that does not upset us, as we do not aspire to it or see it in the same way. But it is within us, as well as in the infinite world separated from us, although we experience ourselves as individuals, as being finite, as something with a beginning and an end.

If we accept the world the way we accept ourselves, we understand the infinity with which we are one. We realize that even without an end, it is not without form; we realize that the world needs no end. The world that has an end – dies, and the world that dies – disappears. The real world cannot disappear. That is why it is infinite. Not because it has no boundaries, not because it has no ends, but because its boundaries and ends are invisible. Its borders and ends exist where we see nothing but emptiness. And where we see boundaries, there are only forms and reflections of infinity in our eyes.

The world should be accepted the way we accept ourselves. In the world, we are with the world. Accepting the world is a victory. The world is a winner in such a conceptualized game and we are doomed to Victory.

TOYS AND MACHINES

THE JUNGLE

Making traps is easier than making new things. Retelling becomes a way – to build oneself by retelling, to remember by retelling, to write down, preserve, and transmit value by deceptive memory.

A remembered tale is often not understood but only well stored. But a stored tale is dead – we know it's there somewhere, yet it is absent. A living tale grows; it grows into us, through us, and is everywhere. It does not live in frequent repetition of old and exotic names or an enumeration of myths, gods, and heroes.

An honest tale is mythology for itself, a cosmos for itself; it transmits and maintains memory, does not tolerate affectation, a manifestation of arrogant learnedness, overpowering through what has been learned; it lives for the sake of genuine knowledge, it is a victory of wisdom, it fights against the letter that displaces the air instead of helping one to breathe, against the image that obscures the vista instead of opening the window; it fights against a victory at all costs, against dull-sensed hunters in the jungle where danger lurks and where the executioner ends up in the hands of the victim, caught in his own trap with which he wanted to catch another executioner.

Everything loses sense when a victim becomes an executioner. Roles change, and no one knows their place – the law of the jungle becomes once again the supreme master and arbiter.

The way back is not that long – the jungle is always close.

A FEW STEPS

Some tales resemble an impassable forest fraught with surprises and traps. If we persevere, at the end of the road, there is a clean landscape, clear water, and sky awaiting us. Being in these tales is not overly pleasant; they require effort as we walk; they lure, seduce, examine, re-examine, and weigh the traveler and the seeker. In these tales, it is never hard to breathe, not even when one exits them after a few steps or returns after half a journey, and a return requires no less effort than the one required to persevere until the end of the tale. (Those who return do not know this.)

When we return and leave the tale, there is no clean landscape, clear water, or sky. The stuffy air awaits and offers a less real, less clear landscape than the one in the tale we left a mere few steps away from serendipity.

THE PARK

Lonesome atop a city slope, and even though everyone knows it, it is never crowded; colors that rarely exist elsewhere, pathways and a pond surrounded with flowers, silence crowned by a nightingale's song. A harmony of colors, sounds, and scents, a heavenly landscape in reach, although rarely visited. If it were not, perhaps this park would not be so divine; it might be less alone but certainly lonelier.

THE VICTORY OF SILENCE

There is little to see or say in the noise – sounds are victorious over words. In silence, there is order and harmony of inaudible notes. These notes await an ear undisturbed by the noise. It is much easier to holler to sell speechlessness and impotence as a word because shouts are no different from one another in the noise.

Not every quietness is silence – sometimes, it is disguised cowardice; neither is every word a tale, but vanity in which it hides. A right word expresses silence, a star captures a right word, and a right word does not name the morning but is an invitation to the morning. A real word virtually needs no words – it ceases to be a word, it ceases to be a naming of reality, and it alone becomes a reality. The right word is a victory of silence.

IT'S A BEAUTIFUL DAY OUTSIDE

A massive cloud of heritage causes anxiety. Between Olympus and Parnassus, to suffocate in the stale air, losing oneself in dark corridors while outside, a beautiful day begs to be lived.

THE POETRY OF THE TOY AND THE MACHINE

Poetry can be good fun – a simple toy for children or a complicated machine for adults. Everyone can find something in it. A problem occurs when adults play as adults or when children grow up, forget how to play, and begin to hate complicated toys and want cheap and simple machines. The game, however, is much simpler than it looks. The problem is not growing up or toys and machines but breaking away from childhood or maturity. Both poetry and toys require a child in an adult and an adult in a child.

JEWELRY AND BOWS

Not everyone enjoys things the same, and those with the most expensive jewelry and shoes always understand the value of a look lingering on a specific detail, a carefully selected bow just for this intended look. Men enjoy abstractions, while women enjoy details.

SYLLABLES AND WORDS

You are watching syllables springing up and looking for their place, looking for meanings in words. As they rush toward life, sparks burst from clumsily arranged sounds, while sparks of illumination glimmer from happily found sounds. You are watching words seeking life in comparisons and onomatopoeias, in metonymies and synecdoches, and you are watching the raped ones, which die in metaphors and those that radiate from an invisible one, which shine like a day without the need to explain it.

Then you wonder if the words are sad, if they are stifled and gloomy in the world of profound ideas. You catch a glimpse of an occasional ironic ray emerging furtively. You wonder where this irony comes from that you didn't aspire to, while the words reply that they have taken care of that part of the job because they still think that laughter is more important than anything, reminding you that you have gone astray. They are setting you back on a slightly more joyful and safer path.

MISCONCEPTIONS AND TRUTHS

Misconceptions help truths open up slowly, like developing petals. Truths taken lightly act like prematurely fermented wine. The truth is ever the same – all-encompassing and omnipresent. However, the journey toward it must be slow; it must come from countless sides. A misconception helps the truth get rid of it.

Both error and misconception give reason to continue; the finally realized truth leads to immobility. Innumerable misconceptions offer innumerable paths; innumerable paths lead toward the truth.

Life divides and extends paths through a multitude of truths. A single path leading toward the one and only truth is the death of the truth. And what is a dead truth worth even if it is a truth?

THE KING

Sometimes, I enjoy it when people bow to me, and sometimes, I get bored with it; everything is at my fingertips, and yet, sometimes, I wish for freedom nourished by effort. A king to everyone in the kingdom, except to myself; when I glance at the naked and old reflection in the mirror, on the bathroom wall, and at the one watching us from inside, I realize that even though clothes don't make a man, they still make a king.

CLOWNS AND KINGS

Who but a court jester can tell the truth to a king? Who can make fun of him or even take over the role of the king for a while? What is the secret of clowns? Why are they forgiven for what others lose their heads? What is this powerless power?

If you are unimportant, your insults are not taken seriously; they become enjoyable. And if you are important, having a sense of humor does not help you, even if you are a genuine clown. You have to be nothing to earn the title of a clown. That title is not earned easily. For so many years, it was not easy for Claudius to play a lunatic.

Something magical connects the king with the clown, a worthless person with the most powerful one. What is the connection between them? Perhaps the king senses the hidden truth in the clown's laughter and words and knows how much boredom lies in the king's dormant heart.

Only powerful and powerless people can be informal with each other. A worthless person reminds the king of their common origin. The king knows how long the path to the throne is, while the clown knows how short the return path can be.

THE FOOLS AND THE RICH

There is one remarkable similarity between fools and the rich. Fools don't know they are not fools, and rich people don't realize they are not rich. Who are those who are rich, then? Probably those who know that property is an illusion, those who can recognize a mad person in themselves, those who know that wealth sleeps somewhere within and that modesty calms the raving mad person who forgets that life, almost accidentally earned, is the only possible reward and wealth.

WISDOM AND SLOWNESS

Since people are not very wise, it is good that they are somewhat slow. Who knows where the agile and the ambitious would take us without wisdom. Being slow sometimes accomplishes the same thing as being wise, only in a different way.

DEJAN STOJANOVIĆ

INVENTIONS

There have been so many epochal inventions, yet things are changing slowly. There have been so many fast and thinking machines, yet somehow things are the same. This, however, is not a reason for concern. Why shorten the road? If we realized all the inventions immediately and all the machines soared, we might reach the end of the road too soon.

ARCHIMEDES

Archimedes's colleague stated that he had already realized the new invention as soon as he saw it.

"If that is so, where's your proof?" Archimedes asked.
"I will prove it to you easily; I only need a little time," the colleague replied.

After a while, Archimedes examined the evidence and exclaimed – "it is wrong."

"How can that be if everything agrees with your result?" asked the colleague.

"It's easy, my dear fellow, I gave you the wrong result. Your proof lags behind your words."

BALANCE

The world is more threatened by those who are too serious than those who are too frivolous and vile. However, it seems everyone has taken this danger too seriously, and now the world is in danger of a lack of seriousness.

The whole problem lies in the balance. Perhaps a balance should not be sought and established among extremes but in details. Without stable elements, the entire building wobbles.

LOGIC

Nothing is more logical than nothing. The most illogical thing in the world is the World. However, nothing is more obvious than the world; that is why we accept it as the greatest truth. Nothing is more obvious than light, nothing more obvious than the darkness that engulfs the obvious; nothing more obvious than the sea and clouds, than rains, forests, and flowers, than sunrises and sunsets, than the Milky Way; nothing more obvious and logical than all living species looking for themselves in the vast sea, dreaming and drinking light as something quite clear. Everything seems so logical: love, the illogical madness of love, and even hatred, evil, and death. How logical the existence appears.

We accept the world because we must; no one chooses life; life chooses itself (us) and imposes itself; life is the very logic. The logic of life is an accomplished fact, imposed knowledge. Logic is the health of life, looking forward to blossoming, growing, movement, and beauty. All that lives is born with knowledge, ability, and the instinct to move and survive. The secret is the final (logicality) on the list of life. No flower is obsessed with mystery but blossoming, which solves the puzzle; a flower is not concerned with causes but beauty and fragrance. The mystery, the logic, and the flower's fragrance all grow from the simple beauty of blossoming, be that logical or not. Only humans are aware of logic – their position is illogical – only humans reach beyond and behind logic while using logic, only humans break laws with the help of those laws.

But how nice it is to be logically illogical and illogically logical; how beautiful it is to accept a gift as the most logical thing to do, and to be and to dream, to bloom and to breathe, like a flower or grass, like a star gleaming until it burns out in the splendor of its logic.

DEATH IS THE GREATEST JUSTICE

The world is life, and life is unrest;
Unrest – hell, and peace – heaven.
The most beautiful deception is life,
And the greatest justice is death.

God sleeps, the Devil creates,
Because the Devil is a God who longs
To gift the hellish fire of life
To the dormant perfection of paradise.

It is easy to be just in paradise
In which both God and the Devil dream the same dream.
The path to paradise is a road to nothing(ness).
Heaven is nothing(ness), and nothing(ness) is death.

THOUGHT AND TOUCH

A MIRACLE

Miracles do exist,
It's only that our eyes are too accustomed
So they don't notice them.

Every new day is a miracle,
A bright dot in an everlasting night.

TOUCH

A look and thought are insufficient.
Genuine thought touches landscapes.
A thought that can touch is complete.
It is a silence that speaks,
Merging with the world.

Touches impregnate the world.

YOUR TALE IS MORE IMPORTANT THAN MINE

I could talk just about anything –
About a drop on a leaf or a deer in the forest,
But I want your tale,
To see you watch a dewdrop,
To see what you see
When you see a deer in the woods.

Your tale is more important.

A SOLUTION

When I used to overthink,
I didn't do quite well.
So, I let the world think (for) me.

I think a lot less now,
And I'm doing much better.

Some solutions are straightforward,
But you recall them too late.

THE WAY OF THOUGHTS

Thought always finds its way. It is not timid; it has more than five senses; it can see the invisible, and it can scent the scentless. It sails lonesome through the wilderness, indifferent to deceptive happiness. It does not chase time – time serves it.

We cannot win the race against time, but we can avoid it.

HEARING

Hearing is more important than rhetoric.
The strongest word means nothing to deaf people.
Fastidious and learned, good hearing births a good word.
Good hearing dislikes noise.
Where there is good hearing, there is order.
Good hearing can sharpen eyesight; it can see with its eyes closed.

THE FORTRESS OF LANGUAGE

In a game of words, you never know who the winner is.
You try to reconcile them;
They overpower you.

You would like to curb the chaos,
It is disobedient and robust.
You won't break me in quickly,
It is telling you.

You're searching for the key,
Trying underground corridors,
But you can't master the language;
The language masters you,
It searches for its spot within you
And breaks free from inside of you.

LOW WIT

Sometimes, low wit is good: it helps one to fantasize about big things.

Thanks to low wit, big businesses are flourishing.

DEFEAT

A truth intended as a means of subjugation – is merely another lie.

If it is not helpful, the truth makes no sense.

Is the truth a sufficiently convincing lie, and a lie – a weak truth?

A lie is not (that) powerful; it is just that no one resists it.

Deceptive achievements lull one to sleep; consent
becomes contagious.

The absolute defeat is not on the battlefield; the real defeat is
consent.

MADNESS

Unlike other animals, humans suffer a lot; animals are often in greater danger, but they are free. Humans are constantly under pressure, even while sleeping. They are more comfortable, but they live imprisoned. Other animals do not suffer from the soul disease – perhaps because they do not have a soul – but they are sincere. There are no lies among animals: a fox is genuine in its cunning; it is her chief weapon. Humans are the only lying beasts (even when they don't have to lie).

ACCORD

Ever since we got tired of inventing, we have been quietly
    roaming.
When we used to seduce one another, we got along well.
How beautiful our tales were – we all believed in them.
Trusted tales have more power than truths that no one notices.

NICE WORDS

Justice, equality, freedom, democracy – these are ordinary words that provoke extraordinary events. Thanks to these lovely words, people shed a lot of blood and buried so much beauty and freedom. Nice words know how to pressure and suffocate justice and liberty. Neither justice nor freedom know how to serve those who offer what they have plundered.

DEMOCRACY

It used to flourish in times of slavery.
It is similar today.

ACTING

Acting is a beautiful stage art, but the whole world is a stage. How can one recognize an actor off stage, a hidden hunter? We flee from seemingly dangerous executioners and voluntarily land in the hands of smiling ones.

MYTHS AND LEGENDS

We have long-buried myths and legends; new myths and legends are being born, and the charm of the unknown from the TV screen offers mystery and unreachable heights. In the buried tales, the peaks offered an embrace; the touch of the height was an ideal, an unattainable goal that redeems itself with a sublimity worthy of the plan. One look was enough, one height to gravitate toward; looks gave birth to looks, and peaks gave birth to heights. Reality grew ever higher.

A BEARDED OLD MAN

He had seen a lot, but he was a man of few words. He had thought about himself and others and understood the speed. He realized that time had not passed because it had passed but because it had been lost.

TRAPS

PHANTASMAGORIA

Some think poetry is easy to write, others believe it is the most challenging thing in the world, and others feel it is neither difficult nor easy. Countless thinkers with their opinions and their experiences with which they would like to change the world. But the world cannot be easily changed, and poetry persists despite the countless opinions, measuring itself on an endless promenade of opinions, forgotten misconceptions, wasting life for thinking, or singing about something with little knowledge but a big desire to say something new. It was just a worn-out flaw disguised in a new opinion, new poetics, new rhetoric, an overly personal truth that nobody understands except for the one who sings about it and which concerns nobody but the one who expresses it.

Countless poetics give birth to countless identical castings. Opinions die in poetics, in poems lost across the deserted cities of a wondrous poetic phantasmagoria.

INTERNATIONAL GLORY

It is enough to write a few lines about tanks in the streets in some sad country, about an apparent injustice, which requires no description; it is enough to move from one side to another, to satisfy someone's taste, the need of the moment, the need for "big" games to take a peek into everything and to prove everything with cheap opinions formed almost on command, almost as a recipe of measured pain to resolve the crisis, to extinguish the pain based on a few words that don't change anything except that they flatter vanity and a misguided interest in all dimensions of life and creation, in the air that is being poisoned by smoke from cars, smoke from the television screens, the smoke curtains of politicians, left and right, the smoke of films and pop culture, smokescreens of intelligentsia that finds an explanation for all this, makes up theories, finds justification for the schizophrenic characteristics of the new rulers, for wars, agreements, contracts; finds reason for obedience, for the sale of beliefs under the disguise of conviction, for several awards, for a few moments of illusion in the hocus-pocus world where the truth does not interest anyone anymore, except for ways for lies to be packaged and sold as the most significant truth with the help of prominent intellectuals that will find a good argument, a good defense and justification for everything. Everything becomes much more comfortable if a hoax is "scientifically" proven.

POLITICAL DISSIDENTS

There are no more dissidents. The cards circulate differently, though they are still not open. No one can quickly move from one side to another; it becomes more subtle, complicated, and dangerous. Seemingly, everything worked out, everything opened up, but some black cloud in the sky always appears suddenly, like every storm or every unpredicted epidemic.

And what to do in a storm when it could not be avoided despite all the precautionary measures, when no dissidents guessed or noticed the direction from which it was coming? – from some unimaginable places, from the head of a madman with a messianic complex, who was waiting for his chance and predicted dormancy of the world and its politicians and dissidents who haven't even noticed that the enemy was not the same and that the whole hostility was a misunderstanding within the same house, the same family, from which the children escaped in different directions, to different ideologies, to different nonsense instilled in by intellectual charlatans and lunatics of previous generations who wanted to change the world and offered a paradise on earth packed in a fight for justice and equality, provided to an innocent, tortured and the crucified human being who had been suffering for thousands of years, not a sledgehammer of exploitation, but a sledgehammer of subtle enslavement in the name of his Being and his salvation, in the name of mercy and equality, in the name of justice, which at one point or another destroyed the nations and sent millions of people to hell. Those who remain alive will stay in the next fifty, hundred, or a thousand years, to be fried in the same nightmare of justice.

LITERARY DISSIDENTS

Almost as a rule, political dissidents were writers, but these were not literary dissidents. Literary dissidents are usually unknown, unnoticed, and ignored by the regime and other writers. They cannot change the side; they cannot change the country or its ideology; they don't belong to movements, don't like advertising; they are not satisfied with temporary achievements, meaningless awards, futile and useless words; they are surprised by the World of big names and a small work, written in large numbers, with the names without value, words that speak thanks to the name but not the story; new stories that build names, and then the story becomes superfluous. A story is just an excuse and a way to make a name that smiles from the covers and admires its glory, overlooking the emptiness where there is a jumble of words without meaning that sing a sad song to the half-deaf ears of those who do not care for the song or the story. The half-deaf becomes a yardstick and an audience. But everything is much more comfortable in the half-blind and the half-deaf world of modern giants that seduce processions of the blind into the world of great emptiness, in whose sky the stars shine and their names live in parallel and independently of their work. In the end, only sad names remain, which no one will remember once others have taken their place, eager for shining glory and their own cover pages. The road between covers is less critical – life is on the surface. It is easier and nicer to dazzle others. And blind people don't care for one or the other, or even the third opinion. They are the best audience; they will be treated according to the formula; it is easy to excite them; it is easy to wake them up from a dream in which they, dull, mute, and helpless, await excitement – another product of the plastic reality, another star-studded name.

BUREAUCRACY

Bureaucracy is a colossal beast; deeply rooted, it exists even among artists; it is an almost losing battle against it. There are too many who are literate, yet too few are smart; people acquire knowledge far too quickly. Through memory to the knowledge on the way to stars that are stepping down to the stuffy rooms of modern bureaucrats, illuminating their ceilings, their horizons where everything is easily resolved by the piles of paper and recipes for how to live, create, run, eat, breathe, learn how to love, how to make love, how to sleep, how to dream, how happiness is achieved under the artificial stars of the new sky that emerged from the bureaucratic rooms of aspiring and impotent minds, unable to love, even though they had all their life to learn what they preach. Yet they forget that love is not a science but an inherent state of mind; they forget animals practice sex without textbooks and that it is not such a secret that requires complete science, courses, and special training. And so impotent, with artificial stars on their rooms' ceilings, become the leading teachers on the way to the stars.

DEJAN STOJANOVIĆ

LITERARY BUREAUCRACY

It fights for membership in associations, juries, editorial offices of periodicals, and literary magazines, and preferably for membership in the academies. It reads a little bit, writes a little, and especially agrees with itself on important moves, important information, important awards, important writers that it plans to enthrone forever in history through a variety of memberships and numerous prizes awarded under the influence of top bureaucrats who know everything, not only about literature but also about secret societies, conspiracies, the Masons that lurk at every corner to crucify someone, steal someone's soul and sell it to an unknown devil, about whom only the chief bureaucrat possesses secret knowledge that he doesn't share; about history, ghosts, missing continents; about who said what to whom in „confidence." Everything passes through the eyes of top bureaucrats who closely watch to ensure that no intruder can enter their ranks and disrupt the order and arrangement of values where everyone knows their place, potential, talent, and position in history.

BESTSELLERS

Anyone who writes can be called a writer because he or she writes. Those who want to become writers attend courses on writing poetry and prose, analyze their own work, and follow other writers' development. Teachers teach them that talent is not required and that anyone who wants to be a writer can do it if they only master the writing technique and the formulas of their chosen genre. One can write a novel in a month with little brainstorming ideas written on the cards and designs and plans on the table. There is no secret; the whole secret is in the technique, a little research, and the rest is solved by form, according to a formula, in which it is all nicely wrapped up and packaged. And so, a bestseller is born.

PARADISE IN TALES

A WEIRD WORLD

When you were handsome, your beauty went unnoticed. Today you are not that beautiful, but people admire your beauty. You think – it is better this way, but your strength is waning; you believe in your beauty less than those admiring it do. You are weird, and the world is even stranger. You accept the game and think to yourself – I am delighted and handsome.

CRYBABIES AND CONQUERORS

The world is divided into those who cry and those who conquer. Crying is easier, though; that's why there are more crybabies. Sometimes it is good to cry, but it is sad to be surrounded by crybabies, even though the conquerors are not much more attractive. Roles cannot be changed. The conquerors will remain robust and ugly; the crybabies will be weak and tender. A weeping conqueror becomes a caricature, a crybaby who would like to conquer – a ridiculous sight. Some simply enjoy crying, while others enjoy conquering. Some like to cry and some to conquer; some turn weakness into a virtue – they earn it through a fight, even if the virtue must suffer.

A HUSTLE

Many find an opportunity in confusion, an opportunity born of storms in a turbulent maze. In peacetime, they question themselves, become enlightened, see themselves better, and others recognize them. In the hustle and bustle, they manage to hide from the confused and busy eyes and even from themselves, finding a way to blame others for their shortcomings, thus turning those shortcomings into virtues.

TIME

How should we judge and evaluate? Have we mastered that skill? What connects us to others, and what separates us from them? What is the source of power or impotence? Who gives whom the right? Who can be sure of their judgment? Who makes mistakes? Who pays the price? Is the judge pondering this? We cannot say that there is no real judge. No one sees or hears him; he weighs and measures imperceptibly.

SHIELD

There is always some icy ray of air passing through and stopping us in our tracks. We begin to think something is wrong with us, and we start looking for answers. What we need is a shield. Neither the highest speed nor the most enthusiastic intentions can save us from the icy ray. We need protection before we set off; every motion is a war.

TEACHERS

Teachers teach you to be good, and you become good. They prepare you for life. Now, others expect something of you. Although seemingly equipped, you feel that you are not; despite being good and full of virtues, you are roaming with unease. You begin to doubt yourself; others ignore you and overlook your virtues while less virtuous people progress. Life started much earlier.

WORDS AND IDEAS

Overused, words are flowing into the sewers. Lonely and deceived words end up in landfills. The remaining ones tremble, alienated from fear, from sobered thoughts that dare not step into the word, from eyes blinded by a too-strong vision, too-strong truths taken for granted. Words also die of sorrow, just like their listeners. In the end, everyone seems to be deceiving everyone else. Nobody has won in this game, while the idea has lost a lot. The word, however, had its chance.

TIME AND VALUE

LIFE AND ART

Is a poem only what resembles a poem – full of references and allusions – to reiterate what has been said too many times before, the history and classical works, and to create art, or is a poem a record of life as if you were alive for the very first time?

GLORY

Gone are the days of cheap rhymes, pleasant deceptions, and intense ecstasies. New passions should count not on the flights of feelings but on the flights they offer. The goal of the tale is not to fly but to inspire flight. However, fame is ever so sweet. Fame is not predictable, which is why Keats calls her a Gypsy. We do not choose it; it chooses us. Thanks to cheap words, this Gypsy rewards many unjustifiably and unexpectedly.

VALUE

What are all these voices fighting for? For their own victory or the victory of their profession? Is my success real? Does the winner with a laurel wreath ask this question? Do I deserve victory, or did I steal it from someone more worthy of victory? Sometimes, it is more victorious to lose than to win. Nevertheless, many are so used to laurels and presume they are real winners. Time, however, often removes the laurel wreaths and places them on the heads of the real winners. Then, usually, both are dead. Most often, adorned winners have not worked for posterity, but the laurel wreaths and real winners do not care about adorned victories. An unrewarded value is more valuable than a reward with no value.

DEJAN STOJANOVIĆ

THE DIFFERENCE BETWEEN A POET AND A VERSIFIER

A versifier arranges words and rhymes into verses; a poet arranges poems and rhymes into meanings.

A sound does not swallow a letter in a real poem, but a letter swallows a sound.

A versifier arranges sounds; a poet arranges meanings in the sounds.

To a versifier, sounds are the means and the aim; a poet travels, using sounds as instruments and servants toward the purpose.

A versifier passes through the sound; sounds go through a poet.

A versifier's poem is born by the sound; the poem maintains a poet's sound.

A poem does not radiate from the name, but the name emanates from the poem.

The name does not create the poem, but the poem brings value and fame to the poet.

NAME AND WORK

There are anonymous poems and poets without poems.

Some works say a lot without fanfare, and some boast through work.

Names, of themselves, do not write poems, nor do they create work.

Names, of themselves, do not know how to sing, although they sometimes sound glorious.

Names themselves may sound nice because no one peeks behind the cover pages to see the sad face of a poem crying for meaning while the author's name proudly smiles from the title.

A poem that is a name to itself does not yearn for the author's name but shines from its name and title alone.

A poem is its own name and cover.

Some only speak, and some dream and show.

Knowing how to dream is more important than the story because the story tells itself. It is easy to arrange the words in a story born out of a dream; a narrative without an invention and a dream cannot help even a story itself.

SALE

Many writers were better before they became famous. A word was more valuable to them; they were unsure of its value. Since they became famous, their word has been more expensive, but their value is less. A well-paid word deceives them. And what kind of a word is a word that has a price, high or low, which the writer adjusts to the cost of fame, and how, long ago, when appreciation of them was less, it was more valuable than it is today with a high price? Words do not choose their company or discriminate among those who use them. We do not know who tricked whom. Did the writer deceive the word, or did the word fool the writer?

NUMBER AND WORD

The number of missing words measures the length of novels, poems, and stories; a thousand pages become one, one becomes a thousand.

The world of numbers and words is odd.

A number is the only word that does not lie.

Words can be very deceitful; they create the illusion that a large number hides a great word.

A number is still very accurate, but its role is changed. In the reversed position, this number enriches the silence.

In its proper function, a number counts the missing words.

A right word counts the silence; the page counts a lousy word.

A word is not filling in the gaps but the fertilization of silence.

Unwritten words grow out of silence.

IN OUR DARKNESS

We think that what we overlook is neither seen nor extant.
Therefore, we ignore it.

We believe that what is not recognized is neither valuable nor does
it exist.
Therefore, we do not recognize it.

We believe that the World depends on us, our decisions, and on
bright recognition.
Therefore, we are the ones who blindly decide.

We prefer blind decisions and recognition to bright
disappointments.
Therefore, we turn off the light.

In the end, we see better in our darkness.
It is nice to be unrecognized in the recognized World.

ABSURDITY

The world is absurd. Although it is obvious – the thought of it exists. Accepting the world resolves the absurdity. Without mystery, there would be no sense; mystery offers both movement and hope; mystery makes movement possible – there is no goal without mystery. At first, the conundrum seems absurd – arranging pebbles solves the puzzle; working on the mosaic is more important than the solution – every stone solves the secret and every stone is an answer. Absurdity arises from the relationship: if the world is accepted – there is no absurdity. Misunderstanding the world is a source of absurdity; understanding is achieved through acceptance; faith is acceptance of the world, one of the forms of understanding; belief resolves the absurdity.

There is no end to the mystery of the human form and the human condition. Mystery can only be vaguely anticipated, illustrated by collusion with the universal essence and merging by the feeling of thoughts and the thought of feelings. Science is of no help in experiencing the world – we cannot learn how to experience; science directs but offers no definitive answers – for there are none.

Nobody can measure the intelligence of feelings, the intelligence of self-sacrifice, or the participation of all great yet nameless people in the world's construction. History is the sum of recorded events; oral tradition has long been gone. All knowledge is a collection of tales; history is memory, recorded memory, and interpretation.

Nobody knows what nourishes the world. Nobody knows precisely how many hoaxes lie hidden behind many great endeavors and outstanding achievements; nobody can measure the value of failure, the value of unrealized talent that has burned out in vain. We do not know or appreciate the value of someone who cared less for the name than for the work and to whom a nameless deed illuminated both the path and fall.

The world does not always work in favor of itself but also against itself. Its value often exists despite the world; everything is in collision. The world is an anthill and a menagerie. The law is the minimal way to bring order into chaos, achieving more of an illusion of order than genuine order.

Who can measure the strength of an ongoing ruse that somebody sold as valuable and successful? Who wrote the history of the tricks? Who is fighting for others? Who has examined how many sadists or masochists have been among the creators of "happiness" throughout history? Who has counted all the psychopaths, quacks, and lunatics, many of whom are still living today in our heads as role models, leaders, and saints? Who has ever written a history of madness (Foucault), a history of sadism, a history of masochism, a history of vanity, a history of hysteria, a history of affectation, a history of philistinism, a history of grief, a history of pain, a history of joy, a history of faith unaffected by religion, a history of love, a history of hatred, a history of goodness, history of evil? Where is a history of grace, physical beauty, the beauty of smiles, the beauty of looks? Where is a history of courage, a history of heroism, a history of cowardice, a history of chivalry, a history of poetry as an act, a history of hope, a history of dreams, a history of construction, a history of cities (Lewis Mumford), a history of conversation? Where is the real history?

Is the theory of evolution the answer to humans or for humans? What does the theory of evolution prove? What is true evolution? Is thought a proof of and a justification for everything? The one thing that sets humans apart from other animals is their memory. However, the memory of a single person or a family is short, and so is the memory of a people. The whole human memory shines from the tale, not from the person. A loss of the story and recorded memory in a single second can bring humans back to the woods.

The value and heroic spirit that gives birth to heroic and sublime thought can be a hope for humans. Every memory is deceptive, and every tale is incomplete. Only an unsullied thought encompasses the whole memory; only a heroic act saves people and saves a person from himself or herself.

Unrecorded history is perhaps the most important. How much do we know about the person who uttered the first word? Who composed the first prayer? Who aspired to the expression and form that earns one contact with the World and a deserved place in the academy and temple of the World, for whose membership no proposal, praise, or diploma is required? Who are the real heroes and builders? As a real heritage, we have only the works occasionally produced and preserved by the labor of love in inspiration. Who explained the intelligence of the senses, the biological intelligence of the body, and its beauty? Some sculptures, paintings, and songs did. Nevertheless, where does the mind sleep? When and how does one wake it up? Who explained that? Who wrote an accurate history of culture, a history of non-culture, a history of anti-culture?

What we read is often not knowledge but data. Knowledge springs from thoughts and not from other people's words. No diploma guarantees thought; no diploma guarantees intelligence. No position guarantees the value of the one who occupies it. Value radiates from itself. Only true thinking can we acquire real knowledge. Who wrote a real history of thought? Who explained what actual knowledge is, true intelligence or true thought? Who understood love for wisdom and how it is born and evolved?

Individuals must deal with their own devices. The seemingly existing order only allows the functioning of the machine dominated by illusion, delusion, and lies. The primary starter of the engine is the relentless life-and-death struggle. The fact that there is not much blood on the streets is no evidence that blood is not running into the world's sewers; it is merely evidence that there is a tender way of killing. Even murder is suitable if people find a proper way. Crime just should not be revealed; if people discover it, one should not allow the possibility of evidence and should cover up the offense with sublime goals and interpretations. The world becomes an interpretation.

Life becomes not life, but an interpretation of life, an acceptance of someone's request or vanity, a defense, not of integrity, but a form presented as an authority. (What do we dream? From most dreams sings the desire for glory; from most works sings a reward and not the deed – all that deceives the song and the world.)

THE SKILL

How much is worth a poem and a tale that nobody reads? How much worth is there in the mastery we overlook? Skill is not only in skillfulness; skill is in communication, in explaining the world we see yet overlook, in explaining the world we do not see but long for, and in discovering what is known in a new vision of what we already saw. Skill is hidden in the invisibly visible, in a smile that passes us by, in a forgotten beauty, in a deceased truth; skill mocks an overslept day, stale air, a novelty at all costs, confusing thoughts, feelings that cry for no reason; skill weeps over the folly of the world that finds joy in anesthesia and does not accept life as a hope, but as a sad deception; skill finds meaning in meaninglessness; out of meaninglessness, it rises and builds castles in the sand regardless of them being in the sand, and builds a city in the void.

HEROISM

The new is not the latest, but the new that grows from the old.

The new is not in lifeless mastery that flirts with vanity and hopes for the impossible.

A novelty at all costs is a stillborn or a sickly child who postpones death.

Unbridled freedom and arrogance are more dangerous than the sentimentality they mock. Arrogance conceals impotence with insolence, while sentimentality counts on someone else's impotence.

A form without purpose is not construction but wandering in vain.

Everything is poetry, but not everything is a poem.

Every subject is worthy of poetry, but not every poem is.

A poem with something to say is a poem, even if not one.
A poem that lulls you to sleep is not a poem, even if it is one.

Everything that enslaves life is a form worthy of life.

Everything that thinks life can be retold and understood with trite mastery is not worth life.

Entering darkness without trepidation is a condition on the path of light.
Entering the unknown to enable oneself is worthy of art.

A poem does not sing from rhymes, but rhymes sing from life.

A painting that does not observe us is not a painting but a dead form on a canvas.

Life is not learned from books – books are mere preparation.

A perfect form is nothing if it conceals a perfect void within.

Only in life is there imperfection.

Sometimes, a mistake helps us live; without errors, life would be too easy, and quickly achieved perfection loses value.

Disciplined freedom leads to gaining sight; a tamed passion leads to understanding; nobility – to wisdom, and the name of nobility is heroism.

WINDOWS

Light does not bring the world into the room
It merely helps one to know what is what

If we name the invisible
We open up both reality and words

If the air does not cleanse the soul
It is of little help that it serves the respiratory organs

If the light does not reach deep into us
There is little benefit from open windows

If we merely pass through the world
We are but lost wanderers in the desert

We are the windows
Of the world visiting us

Knowing what is what is more important than naming
Words offer not life, but explanations

We can never correctly name the world
Through experience, we name the world

When the world breathes us, we name the world
Experience is the name of the world

When light departs from the window of our eye
Light moves into us

When the world dreams of us, we dream of the world
The path of the world is an inward path

IDEAS

Everything boils down to a mere few words, a few primary concepts. All that remains are tales that serve them.

Notes on the Poems' Creation Dates

The poems written between 1996 and 1999:
The "Toys and Machines" cycle: "Death is the Greatest Justice."
The "Thought and Touch" cycle: "Miracle," "Touch," "Small Mind," "Defeat," "Madness," "Harmony," "Nice Words," "Democracy," "Acting," "Myths and Legends."

Poems written in 2001:
The "Thought and Touch" cycle: "The Bearded Old Man."
The "Paradise in Tales" cycle: "The Strange World," "Weepers and Invaders," "The Crowd," "Time," "The Shield," and "Teachers."

Poems written in 2007:
The "Toys and Machines" cycle: "Logic."
The "Time and Value" cycle: "Absurd."

The rest of the book was written in 2008.

ABOUT THE AUTHOR

Dejan Stojanović was born in Peć in 1959. He graduated from the Law School of the University of Priština. He has published these books of poems:

Circling (Krugovanje), Narodna knjiga – Alfa, Belgrade, three editions – 1993, 1998, and 2000.

The Sun Observes Itself (Sunce sebe gleda), NIP Književna reč, Belgrade, 1999.

The Sign and Its Children (Znak i njegova deca), Prosveta, Belgrade, 2000.

The Creator (Tvoritelj), Narodna knjiga, Belgrade, 2000.

The Shape (Oblik), Gramatik, Podgorica, 2000.

The Dance of Time (Ples vremena), Konras, Belgrade, 2007.

Pentalogy: *The World in Nowherness (Svet u nigdini):*

1. Ozar (Ozar), Udruženje književnika Srbije, Belgrade, 2017.

2. The World and God (Svet i Bog), Udruženje književnika Srbije, Belgrade, 2017.

3. The World in Nowhereness (Svet u nigdini), Udruženje književnika Srbije, 2017.

4. The World and Humans (Svet i ljudi), Udruženje književnika Srbije, Belgrade, 2017.

5. The Home of Light (Dom svetlosti). Udruženje književnika Srbije, Belgrade, 2017.

The Hidden Light (Skrivena svetlost), Čigoja, Belgrade, 2018.

Primordial Spark (Iskra iskona), Albatros plus, Belgrade, 2021.

Centuries and Steps (Vekovi i koraci), Albatros plus, Belgrade, 2023.

Essays:

Creator and Creating (Stvaralac i stvaranje), Albatros plus, Belgrade, 2021.

The New Man and the New World (Novočovek i novosvet), Rad, Belgrade, 2022.

Anthology: *Selected Serbian Plays* (*Izabrane srpske drame*), USA, 2016.

Philosophy: *Absolute*, New Avenue Books, USA, 2024.

A book of his selected interviews, Conversations, was published in 1999 by NIP Književna reč, Belgrade. The Serbian Heritage Foundation and the Association of Writers of Serbia for Intellectual Engagement awarded the book the Rastko Petrović Prize.